KNUCKLEHEAD FRED

Arias Williams

BANDELE
— BOOKS —

Publisher: Bandele Books
Interior Design: Antoine Bandele
Original Concept Art: Alvin Harvey II
Illustrator: Bolaji Olaloye
Cover Design: Miblart

ISBN: 978-1-951905-89-7
Hardback, Second Edition | April 30, 2020

For Gaia & Heru

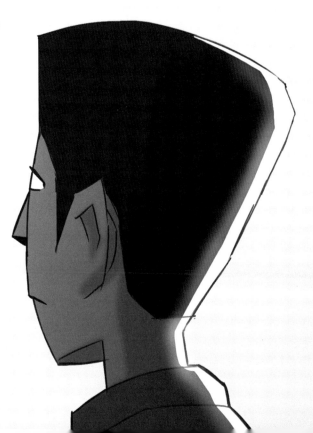

"Or when we asked you to eat your veggies? Not a lot. Just some!"

"Or in the family photo, we just wanted you to smile.

But, no, instead you gave us your most spiteful scowl!"

"That's not good in our book.
Good kids do what they are told.
We're your parents, we love you,
it's not that we want to control.

We only want what is best,
to protect you from harm.
To make sure you're well-nourished
and don't have stinky underarms."

Fred listened, tears running from his eyes.

He said,
"I guess I haven't been good,
I just never realized.
I promise I'll be better,
I'll listen. I swear."

"I'll eat my veggies,
I'll walk everywhere!
So can I have a dollar,
please, please?
The line is getting short,
the ice cream truck
is going to leave."

Mother said, "Not today. Fred, you have to prove what you say. If I give you money, you'll forget by the end of the day."

Fred stormed off
at the tip of a rage!

He nearly blew his cool,
acting many years below his age.

Alone in his room
he was stewing in fury.

Fred said, "It's just one dollar!
I can't believe this is how they do me."

As usual, Fred began to ignore, but then he remembered his promise and hopped to his feet. He cleaned his entire room, and even changed his sheets.

Later that evening, while playing video games with the volume on blast, his mother asked...

"Can you put that on pause and take out the trash?"

The very next day when Fred was home, and after school work was finished, he heard the ice cream truck ringing, and his excitement was replenished.

He ran to Mom and Dad, and dropped down to his knees. His Father pulled out a dollar and said, "Spend as you please."

Fred was so happy that he jumped for joy. Mom said, "You always get what you want when you've been a good boy."

ABOUT THE AUTHOR

Arias Williams is a creative based
in Los Angeles, California.

He is a Father of two children,
a husband, and currently teaches
7th Grade in South Los Angeles.

When he isn't working on Knucklehead Fred,
Arias can be Found in his home studio making beats,
hanging with his Family, or working to educate
the Future of Los Angeles.

A NOTE FROM THE AUTHOR

THANK YOU FOR READING KNUCKLEHEAD FRED,
I SINCERELY HOPE THAT YOU AND YOUR FAMILY ENJOYED IT!
THE IDEA FOR THIS BOOK CAME TO ME AFTER A FAMILY OUTING WITH MY OWN CHILDREN,
WHO WERE MISBEHAVING AWFULLY. ALL I COULD THINK ABOUT WAS HOW
THEY WERE ACTING LIKE A COUPLE OF KNUCKLEHEADS.

MODELED AFTER SOME OF MY FAVORITE MISCHIEVOUS CHARACTERS
FROM LITERATURE AND TELEVISION, I COMMITTED TO WRITING THIS BOOK
IN ORDER TO ADD TO THE GROWING GENRE OF CHILDREN'S BOOKS
CENTERED AROUND BLACK CHILDREN AND FAMILIES.

IF YOU AND YOUR CHILD ENJOYED KNUCKLEHEAD FRED,
PLEASE CONSIDER LEAVING A REVIEW ON YOUR FAVORITE RETAILER
OR SOCIAL MEDIA PLATFORM.

Lightning Source UK Ltd.
Milton Keynes UK
UKRC011013080620
364496UK00001B/5